I0596165

A thin line between LOVE & FEAR

(Unravel Series)

A thin line between LOVE & FEAR
(Unravel Series)

Erica T. Capri

Gemlight Publishing LLC.

Gulfport, Mississippi

A thin line between LOVE & FEAR(Book Two
of "A Thin Line" Unravel Series

ISBN:**978-17344326-3-3**

1st Edition ISBN: **978-1-7344326-7-1(Book One
of "A Thin Line " Unravel Series**

Design by : Erica Sherrill

Printed in the United States of America

This book is dedicated to everyone who

supported my writing endeavors.

A thin line between LOVE & FEAR

(Unravel Series)

Erica T. Capri

Prologue

Years have passed by like a whirlwind. My daughter Destiny was born and now has grown up to be a gorgeous little princess. All the wounds from my broken marriage and the incident with Scott have faded away.

My life has become God's and Destiny's world, doing things to please Him and cherishing moments with my daughter.

I've spent a lot a time throughout the years traveling, doing full time ministry and motivational speaking with my women's group, Destiny's Will. God has opened so many doors for me to travel and explore the world, and to help so many women in dealing with depression, domestic violence, abuse, and relationship struggles. Scott and I have developed close friendship for the sake of our daughter.

My baby girl Destiny is now two years old. Every day I'm breathing I am thanking God that I could see her grow, see her first steps, and hear her first words. Destiny is my miracle. After multiple miscarriages, struggling with depression, and doctors telling me that it was impossible for me to carry a child, let alone deliver one without problems, I was blessed with the perfect baby girl. I am so honored and grateful to have Destiny, and to carry and deliver her without complications. She has the most beautiful curly hair, brown eyes, bronze skin, and the voice of an angel. To me, her hugs are worth more than millions of dollars. Every second I'm without my little princess, traveling for work or something, breaks my heart until I can see her again. Now it's summertime, and I have a women's event in New York that will require me to stay for a week. During that time, I know I'll need strength while I'm away from my baby, but the little freedom will give me a little 'Me Time'.

Chapter One

I was awakened by Scott yelling from downstairs and Destiny jumping on the foot end of my bed.

"Kendall, you up? It's 8am, your plane leaves in an hour and a half."

"Yes," I called back as I jumped out the bed and rushed into the bathroom. Destiny followed me, pulling on me while she wrapped her little arms around my legs. Scott came in the bathroom a few moments later, while we were brushing our teeth.

He quickly grabbed Destiny to get her dressed, lifting her up and swinging her around like an airplane. Like always, Destiny's eyes lit up, her little smile glowing in delight. I do love to see their relationship grow.

I quickly made my way to the shower. After letting the warm water run over my body, I got out of the shower and slipped on some comfortable clothes for the plane trip.

Rushing downstairs to the kitchen to grab something for Destiny to eat, Scott had already fed and dressed her while waiting on me to finish getting dressed.

"You ready, woman?" Scott asked as he picked up Destiny and headed out the door.

"Yes, let me grab my granola bar and orange juice." I replied easily.

"Okay, we will be waiting in the car."

After twenty minutes' drive, I finally reached the airport. Scott and I got out of his car and I walked over to get Destiny out of her seat. Making my way to the entrance of the airport, Scott handed me my bags. I glanced down to check my watch—a quarter till nine. I had less than ten minutes to make it to my flight gate.

"Well, it's time for me to get going."

"Okay Sweetie, be safe." Scott replied. He wrapped his arms around me, hugging me lightly and patting my back once before quickly withdrawing. "Call me as soon as you get settled."

"Yes, I will, I really appreciate you keeping her while I'm gone."

"You're welcome, no problem Kendall. Destiny's my child too, you just enjoy yourself and don't work too hard."

"Thanks," I replied, flashing a smile at Scott as I departed from him. Walking over to Destiny, she ran over, wrapping herself around my leg again. I just love when she does that, so I awkwardly bent over and gave her a big hug and kisses on the cheek. Destiny pecked me on the cheek and whispered that she loved me in my ear, melting my heart. Catching myself from crying, I grabbed my bags and walked into the entrance of the airport. I looked behind to wave my final goodbye to them, catching sight of Destiny trying to run to me from a distance, crying. I couldn't bear to see her cry for me, so I didn't turn back around.

Finally, I made my way past all of the gates except mine. Pressed for time and not knowing where my gate entrance was, I started getting a little aggravated, so I went to ask the receptionist how to get to my destination. She pointed me to the right direction and warned me quickly that I had less than a minute to make it to the gate before it closed. I rushed toward the gate, bags falling and hair everywhere; looking from the distance I saw the gate closing slowly.

"Hold the gate, please!" I screamed, running to reach the doors. Thankfully, the attendant heard me and held the gate open until I made it to the doors. I gave her my ticket, took a deep breath and made my way onto the plane. As I entered the plane, all eyes were on me. Everyone was looking at the woman who had nearly missed the flight, making it awkward for me as I scrambled to my seat. Finally, I made it to my seat, finding it mercifully empty. "Thank God." I placed my bags in the cubby above my seat; I sighed with the relief of making on the flight and having a seat all to myself.

Hearing the announcement of the pilot about the impending departure, I laid my head against the chair and said a silent prayer. Opening my eyes, there was an attractive tall man standing looking at me. He had bronze skin, a shaggy beard, and curly hair tapered on one side with deep dark brown eyes. He had an amazing body, which took me into a daze. He cleared his throat to get my attention.

"Excuse me, I believe this my seat," he said with an easy smirk. I started looking around to see if he was really talking to me.

"I'm sorry, did you say this is your seat? You must have read the wrong seat number. See, I don't have anyone sitting with me, which is perfect after the morning I've had so far, so can you please find your seat so this plane can get moving?"

"I'm sorry that you're having a bad day, but this is my seat; B-12." He reached over and showed me his ticket that did, in fact, read seat B12. I wanted to just scream and get off the plane. Just when I thought things would go smoothly.

"I'm Connor Collins, and I'm here to listen all about how your day was so bad." He replied, and then sat down in the seat beside me smiling. I glanced over at him at a loss for words, thinking in my mind that this is going to be the longest ride ever.

Quickly, I reached to grab my phone off the seat, and plugged in my headphones.

Chapter Two

Finally, our plane was taking off, and suddenly two warm hands grabbed my thighs, holding on tight. Connor seemed to be having flying phobia.

"Oh, my gosh! You scared me! Can I have my thigh back please?"

"Wait, please bear with me." Connor replied while still holding my thighs in a tight grip.

"Are you going to be okay? "I asked him as I glanced at his horrified face.

"Yes, just flying is not my thing." After about five minutes of turbulence, the plane started to fly smoothly and then Connor released my thighs. At that very moment, I was getting lost in my thoughts on what God's purpose was with this encounter. Connor gazed into my eyes and flashed me a smile. "Glad you didn't slap me."

"Trust me, it was my first instinct until I saw the fear in your eyes."

He grabbed my hand. "Well, thank you, Ms...?"

"Ms. Kendall Alexandra, you can just call me Ken or Kendall whatever your preference." We then shook hands.

"I think I like Kendall. Thank you, Kendall for being patient with me. Oh, and don't judge me, no sugar in my tank I'm all man." He said with a smirk on his face.

I began to really consider his face for the first time, staring, not just a glance. Connor was very attractive despite the messy beard that looked like he hadn't shaved in a month. Then he had that accent in his voice that was amazingly attractive. I chuckled. "I'm sure, but I didn't need to know all that extra information. Besides, what make you think I will judge you, I believe everyone fears something in life.

" He chuckled at me, and then we chattered non-stop on the plane until I dosed off to sleep.

Suddenly, my body was spreading across the horizon, a big field covered with colorful, beautiful flowers all around me. Bewildered as to how I'd gotten there, I began to look for a path. In the far distance of the field, there were two little girls playing. When I saw them, I began to get a little closer while looking to find pathways to get to them. As I got closer, one of the little girls looked more and more like my baby girl Destiny and the other little girl looked similar too. They seemed to be one year apart.

Out of nowhere a man's hand came and grabbed mine, guiding me to the little girls. When I was several feet away, I recognized that one of them was Destiny.

But the other little girl wasn't close as I thought to us. The nearer I tried to get to her, the more distance appeared between us. She started yelling, Momma help me. Feeling perplexed trying to figure out why I couldn't reach her, I began to run and try to get her. Eventually she disappeared, though, which brought my heart to sadness. Trying to get answers, I called the man who was guiding me, "Hello!"

The man didn't answer.

"Can you hear me?" He still didn't answer, and then I felt myself getting aggravated. "Hello! Hello!"

"Kendall? Kendall! Hello!"

"Hello, can you hear me?" I replied, but the sound of that voice calling my name sounded a lot like Connor, and it was very close to my ear. Suddenly I was shaken by a strong force. When I opened my eyes, there was Connor staring me right in the face, and the plane had landed at the New York City Airport. I had been deep in a dream that seemed so real.

"It's time to go beautiful, are you okay? It seems like you were in a deep dream."

"No, I dreamed about my little girl and another little girl that looked a lot like Destiny. They were playing in the field, then this guy came and guided me on a path to get to them, but when I got close it was only my daughter and the little girl was so far away and she was calling me Mommy. I think God is showing me that I'm going to have a little girl or adopt one."

"Wow, that was a vivid dream, and you have no idea who the little girl was?"

"No, she looked so much like Destiny." I said as I scratched my head, thinking on the purpose of the dream.

"Okay, I'm sure God will guide you to resolve your dream, but we have to get off this plane before they escort us off with security. Do you need help with your bags?" Connor asked as he grabbed his bag.

"No, I think I can manage."

"Kendall, it's okay to accept help," he said, looking at me and raising his brows.

"No really, I can manage, it's not that many." Connor reached over my head and grabbed two of my bags.

"Okay," I sighed and looked over at him. He shook his headed, smiling, then we exited the plane. Walking to the entrance of the front door, I searched for my phone to call for an Uber driver so I could get dropped off at the hotel.

"Where are you staying at?" He asked as he followed me to the door.

"Four Seasons Hotel downtown."

"Really? That's where I 'am staying too, up on the 16th floor. You're more than welcome to ride with me since we are headed in the same directions."

With no hesitation I rejected his offer, and walked outside on the busy sidewalks of New York. Standing on the sidewalk several people bumped into me, beggars on the corner, prostitutes across the street. That's when it clicked in my mind that I'm not in the country--I'm in the largest city in United States. Being alone I would need to be very careful, even though I know God is covering me. I thought that maybe He was using Connor to cover me from danger while I'm here. I looked over at Connor and he was looking at me, dragging his hands through his beard.

"What?" I said to him with a wavering voice and avoiding eye contact.

"Nothing, it's just now I have to figure out what I'm going to do with you. First let's talk about making a deal, Ms. Kendall. I will not ask you out for dinner if you ride with me to the hotel. I know these streets and they are dangerous; besides, I will have a sense of ease if you ride with me. That way I'll know you're safe" I cringed and stared at the busy streets with a slow, disbelieving shake to my head.

"Seriously, you are using this 'I want to keep you safe' game to get me to ride with you?"

"Yes, but no, see I really want you to ride with me and I definitely want you safe." He stammered.

"No dinner, right?" I asked while I was observing him.

"No ma'am, no dinner, and matter of fact, once we arrive at the hotel, we can go our separate ways, but--"

I stopped him before he finished. "But, but what?" I asked sarcastically, heartbeat quickening.

"But if we bump into each other again, you must go to dinner with me, because that will be fate." He replied, displaying a wide grin.

"No way, you know we will bump into each other again."

"No, I don't, it's a huge hotel--about 52 floors and 400 rooms, you have your own schedule and agendas, which make it impossible. So, is it a deal or not?"

Taking a step back, feeling overwhelmed and ready to make to the hotel so I can relax, I looked over at Connor and gave him wide smile.

"Mmmhmm. All right, it's a deal. So, there we have it, once we get to the hotel, we will go our separate ways, and if we happen to bump into each other again, I owe you dinner?"

"Yes, and a kiss." He said, turning away and bursting out in laughter. My eye squinted at him, lit with an inner glow. I just chuckled and we climbed into the car he reserved. At that moment, I could feel my pulse in my throat. Every nerve in my body was working overtime.

****

Chapter Three

After fifteen minutes of riding through the streets of New York City, we had finally arrived at the Four Seasons Hotel. The building was so huge. At 682 feet tall and 52 stories, it is the second tallest hotel New York City and the fourth tallest in the U.S. We parked the car and I was about to open the door, but Connor jumped and beat me to the passenger side.

"Let me get it for you," he replied, staring me in the eyes as he swung open the door for me.

"Thank you, but you don't have to do this." I said as I flashed him a smile.

"It's in my nature to treat every woman as a queen. I was raised by my grandmother who taught me all the right ways of being a gentleman." He said as he looked at me, escorting me out of the car. We walked into the beautiful luxury entrance of the hotel. Connor sat my bags down near me while gazing into my eyes.

"I'm a man of my word, so I believe this is it unless God sees different," he responded as he laid down my last bag.

"Yes, it is, you take care of yourself Connor." I was hit with a desire to move closer to him, hug him, kiss him on the cheek or something. Thinking I may never see him ever again, at least I got closer to this amazingly attractive gentleman. It was just something different about Connor I had never seen in a man. Connor wasn't the normal male type, he was honest and unique in his own ways that I admire about him.

I grabbed my bags and headed toward the front desk to get my room reserved. Seeing him walk off a distance going the opposite direction, he stopped and looked back at me like he had lost something dear. We engaged steady contact until I waved goodbye. He waved back smiling my way to my room my phone started ringing.

I fished in my purse to find it and, picking it up, noticed a picture of Scott on my screen, notifying me that I had an incoming Skype video. I pressed accept as I was positioning the key card inside my room door. I finally entered my room, laid down my bags and looked at my phone to see Scott and Destiny on the video. There my baby girl was smiling in the camera with her face filled with cake frosting that her grandfather gave her. Giving Destiny a warm smile in the camera, Scott bent over in the camera smiling.

"Hey, how was the trip?" He asked as he stared at me through the video.

"It was great, actually. I just made it to my room when you guys were calling." Destiny moved toward the camera trying to kiss it.

"Love you," she said in her innocent voice. While she kept trying to kiss the camera, Scott stopped her and told her she couldn't, so she started giggling, making us laugh at her silliness.

We chatted for about an hour, and then it wasn't long before Destiny was fast asleep, and Scott left her room. Scott and I talked for another thirty minutes about how Carol and him being on bad terms. I prayed for him, and then we hung up the phone. After a few hours, I could get some dinner, take a warm shower and complete some work for the conference. Just as I got my eyes shut good and tight, there was a knock at my door. I got up and groaned, dragging myself to the door. Not thinking to check through peek hole in the door, I just opened it and lord behold the person who was on the other side of the door was not what I was expected. It was Larry.

Chapter Four

"Relax Kendall, please don't go bizarre on me. Just let me explain why I'm here." Larry said as he tried to approach me. I grabbed the door to slam it closed, but he pushed it open with his hands. Fearing that life events would start repeating themselves, my first action was to start yelling for help. Larry hurried up and grabbed me, forcing himself into my room. He locked his arms around my shoulder trying to get me to calm down.

"Kendall, I'm not here to hurt you, please relax." He whispered in a soft calm tone.

"Don't tell me to relax, you're trespassing. I don't want to be anywhere near you," I snapped as I tried to break loose of his restraining hold.

"Kendall, I'm here to tell you something very important that you will want to know."

"I don't want to know anything about you or your life. How did you know I was here?" I yelled back at him. He slowly pulled away from me looking into my eyes. "Kendall, I've been tracking you since the divorce for many reasons. One is that I'm dying," Larry said quietly, teary eyed, wanting me to feel sorry for him.

I just nodded my head. "Yes okay, why are you here telling me? We are divorced, I'm not your wife anymore and you have no right to keep track of me. What are you, an obsessed manic?" I replied.

He looked over at me and began to walk toward the door. "Yes, you're right, but it's the right thing for you to know, in case I leave you some of my possessions."

Forgetting words to say, I felt pain in the back of my neck while I was trying to articulate my thoughts. Feeling my body getting overheated, I ordered Larry to get out immediately before

I called security to my room.

"That's insane, you are insane, please get out now." I yelled as I pushed him all the way out the door. He stopped walking and turned toward me.

"You hate me that much, you're too naïve to see I'm trying to give you my estates?"

"I don't hate you, I just don't want anything from you. Please stay away from me." I slammed the door and locked it, and then I swiveled away thinking to myself. I flopped on the sofa in the suite and dosed off to sleep.

The weekend was now over, and I hadn't heard from Larry anymore or even bumped into handsome Connor. So, it was time to get to starting day one of the women's conference. I was so excited about the move of God and how this conference could impact millions of women across the country. I went on my daily routine, calling Scott, talking to Destiny, praying, showering, eating and the list goes on. When I finished dressing up, I went to get on the elevator to go to the 4th floor where the Meet and Greet hall reception would be at. As I stepped to get on the elevator, there was a familiar face I knew.

He was Larry's 5'4, shaggy haired, brown eyed, macho Uncle Mason. I walked into the elevator knowing exactly what to expect.

Mason was like a Mafia Godfather type of guy; he had connections and he treated me like his own daughter. There was never a time I couldn't call him and not get anything from him. He told me several times to leave Larry because he knew the type of guy Larry was. When he came around ,it was usually something very serious, because he was a busy man and if it wasn't worth his time he wouldn't bother. Mason threw his arm over my shoulders. "Hello, hot stuff."

My face flushed and he grinned at me. He leaned over and stared at me, then I sighed. "Hey Mason, so good to see you. Did Larry send you here?" I turned to look at him, observing his actions. He shook his head.

"Yes, Larry is really in some deep waters; he has to tell you some important things that you'll want to know. Baby girl, I need you to let go of all what he's done to you and just hear him out this time." He said as he looked at me with sincerity. I knew then that for him to get involved, it must be important.

"I'm sorry, I just can't do it." I said as I exited the elevator. He rushed off following me, and then he stood in front of me and lifted my chin.

"Please Kendall, it's a child involved with this, do it for me and the child." He put his arms around me, embracing me with a tight hug. At that moment I was totally lost for words. My thoughts had every intention to leave and tell him to go to Hell with Larry, because I was at the point in my life where I wanted my past to be the past and move forward. Now they're coming to me about this innocent child that Larry committed adultery on me with. But my spirit wouldn't let me possess that. So, I told him that I would meet with Larry later. He gave me the address to Larry's office, which was two blocks down from my hotel, then kissed me on the cheek as he walked away, reminding me not to hesitate to call him for anything.

I rushed to the meet and greet hall. As I entered the room it was filled with business-men, entrepreneurs, councilmen, teachers and a whole host of women. I was immediately met at the door by the host who guided me to my seat. Once I was seated and started surveying around at the crowd, looking from a far distance there I saw a man walk from behind the stage curtain, a light shining so bright over his handsome face. A look of disbelief crossed my face; it was Connor Collins.

****

Chapter Five

Everything in my world stopped. I never thought I would meet him again. I stared at him as he walked toward the stage with a microphone in his hand. He was beyond handsome. He had cleaned up his beard, it was cleaned shave and shaped, he had on a well-tailored brown blazer with his bulging muscles showing, navy blue slacks and a cream-colored shirt. There was a glow on him that I never seen in a man. His eyes were so deep that they could pierce a soul by looking right at them. I gripped my bag and stood up to walk toward the exit door before he saw me.

Confused thoughts raced through my brain. Why am I running, why I had to see him again, why he at the conference I'm supposed to speak at every night with a microphone in his hand. Who is he?

While I was pondering those thoughts, an angelic male voice was singing from the meeting hall. I stopped and turned around, peeking in the room. I was certainly not expecting him to be the guest vocalist of the conference. As I thought about it a little longer, it came all together.

I just stood still, absorbing all my thoughts and information and listening to his amazing voice. The more I listened to his voice the weaker I got, his tone was calm.

For the rest of the day, I avoided him. I made sure he didn't see me at all. I wasn't sure why I was trying to avoid him because any other woman will run after a man like him. An amazing, handsome, gentleman that honors all women as queens. But for me I just wasn't ready, I guess.

Later that day I caught a cab to meet with Larry at his office. Once I arrived there, I was escorted upstairs into his private meeting hall. His secretary seated me and offered me coffee. Once I sat there for a good five minutes, I started thinking about leaving and forgetting everything.

Just when my thoughts started to turn into my actions, Larry walked into the room.

"I'm glad you came, you look beautiful Kendall," He said as he shut the door behind him, walking toward a seat to sit across from me.

"You're welcome, just get straight to the point and tell why you have me here."

"Okay, just please give me five minutes."

"Five minutes starting now." I said as I frowned up at him. He reached over into a bag and handed me over some papers.

"Here, take these and read them."

"I don't have time to read this, explain to me what it is." I returned shortly, looking down at the papers.

"They are papers to all my businesses, homes and cars. Pretty much everything I own. I want you to have it, I have prostate cancer and it is spreading throughout my body. The doctor is not giving me long to live."

Looking up at him, he was staring at me with fear in his eyes, and his face was almost expressionless. I didn't know what to say at that moment.

"Why me Larry, you owe me nothing."

"Yes, I do, I owe you my life. Kendall, I've done so much damage to you then you can imagine. There's something else I have to tell you." While he was talking my phone started ringing. I stood up and walked toward the door, looking at the phone. It was Scott's picture flashing across my screen.

"I'm sorry, I have to take this." Immediately, I answered the call and talked to my baby girl for ten minutes. Once I finished hanging up the phone, I turned around and looked toward the room where Larry was. All I could see was Isabella yelling at Larry, throwing bags and shoving a beautiful innocent little girl into his arms. Larry sat the little girl down in the chair and pushed Isabella out the door He glanced over and saw me looking at them. I quickly rushed toward the opposite way to get as far away from him as possible. I wasn't ready for this situation, facing all of them at one time. Gasping for air, I gripped hold of the receptionist desk. Larry started yelling my name for me to come back.

"Why?" I asked him as I tried to regain my strength. "Please let me explain." Larry replied as he walked toward me. The little girl jumped out the seat and ran over to me hugging tight to my legs.

"Mommy! Mommy!" She yelled as she gripped tighter. She had beautiful long hair, brown eyes, bronze skin, and looked to be three years old. Innocent as she can be, I felt the urge to embrace her as my own, but I flinched away and slapped Larry.

"Go back to Hell you bastard." Walking away my face was reddened, and my temper was flared.

"How could you play with this little girl's heart like that, you're just sick evil and everything that happen to you, is a harvest of your evilness." Larry just stared at me with emotions in his eyes.

"Kendall, she's your daughter, I've been showing her pictures of you since she was born. I'm sorry but this is your blood." I start fanning myself trying to calm my nerves, but I just couldn't get a hold of it. I reached over and grab hold of a vase off the receptionist desk and slammed it to the ground.

"If you come near me again, it will be the last day you'll be breathing." I yelled with all the anger that was left inside my body.

Suddenly Larry rushed over and grabbed his daughter, sending her with his secretary until

I got out of clearance. Once I made it out of the door and jumped into a cab, he started chasing it trying to stop me. As I was riding in the cab every possible thought came to my mind. The main thought was, how could she be my baby and I didn't carry her.

Chapter Six

After riding around town running my cab bill up, I finally got the cab driver to stop in front of a coffee shop that wasn't too far from the hotel. I proceeded to pay the driver, then walk into the shop. It was super packed. People were jammed together, workers shouting orders with other people coming in and others leaving. It seemed to be one of the busiest and most popular shops.

Pushing my way through the crowd, I found a seat in the near back corner by a window. I sat down, and then took a deep breath.

Trying to gather all my thoughts, I picked up my phone to Google the possibilities of having a child without giving birth. After surfing for a couple of second this page appeared about surrogacy, then stolen sperm. Once I read the articles, I start to have flashbacks on the time when Larry and I kept going back and forth to the fertility doctor and was it a time when an open window where my eggs could have been stolen.

My heart started pounding and I was feeling dizzy. If anyone looked at me hard enough, they would have thought I was about to faint.

Snapping back from my thoughts, I knew this was a serious situation and if it was true, I was going to make sure that my rights were respected and justice was delivered, no matter what it took. It took a moment, but I remembered that Scott's Aunt is a lawyer, and she could answer some question for me. His aunt's name was Azalea Wood; she was the most polite, realistic, sensible short woman anyone will ever meet. She lost only three cases out of 20 years in law. So, if there was anyone, I knew that would know any kind of possible cases, it would be her. Immediately I dialed Scott's number to get him on the phone.

After two rings, he picked up.

"Hey, you." He answered with excitement.

"Hey, I didn't call to talk to Destiny right now, I need a big favor from you." I said with determination and urgency in my voice. Scott knew then I was in some type of trouble.

"Yes, Kendall no problem, what is it?" I can tell in his voice he was getting worried that I was in trouble.

"Can you get in contact with your Aunt Azalea? I need her to call me immediately about a possible case." With that I ended the phone call after I was sure he would contact her.

Once I ordered my coffee, I then left the shop and headed back to the hotel. I nibbled my hands nervously, waiting on the phone call. My mind was clouded with fear. What if she's my child? How will I tell Destiny? What if Larry tries to take her from me again? What if he tries to do something to me? So many thoughts were constantly racing through my mind. Snapping me out of my train of thoughts, my phone started ringing. It was an unfamiliar number. I knew it had to be Aunt Azalea. I paused and sat on a bench that was outside the hotel. We greeted one another and talked about Destiny, then we went into the conversation about Larry. After talking on the phone with her a good thirty minutes, she explained that there is a theft allegation with a fertility case. That women's eggs can be stolen and used to impregnate other woman who later gives birth as their own. They do so by taking eggs without consent, giving patients an unapproved fertility drug and telling them it's a drug to produce fertilization.

I was feeling devastated and remembered when I was given a lot of drugs and that the doctor at the time was a close friend of Larry's family. Knowing Larry, he could've paid him off to do such a crime. She closed our conversation telling me that through the years of her doing consultations, she knew without a doubt based on my facts that my embryos had been used to impregnate another woman without my consent and for Larry to come to me and confess, either the child was probably sick or he knew that if something were to happen to him, the child will need her biological mother. There would be nothing the surrogate or other woman could do because the child isn't hers.

Bursting out with a cry, every bone in my body felt like I was getting stabbed. Entering the hotel lobby, I rushed toward the elevator. Reaching in my purse to find my room key, the elevator thankfully opened quickly. As I looked up to watch the direction of my steps, Connor was standing inside the elevator staring me directly in the face. He looked up and saw that it was me, and I could literally see his eyes glow.

"Wow what a coincidence, we meet once again." He said with a smile on his face. At that point my face was full of tears; I was still in a state of shock. I just stood there and couldn't speak a word while he was holding open the elevator. Connor immediately changed his whole approach. He then stepped out of the elevator, grabbed me gently, and hugged me. While in that moment I just stood there, not having any compassion, or strength to hug him back. I didn't understand, as if my brain short-circuited and needed to be rebooted. Everything was in slow pace while I was motionless in the middle of it all. How could this happen? During this whole time, as I was sobbing feeling terrifically upset, wronged, he was trying to comfort me not even knowing what was going on. It was maybe five minutes later I gasped and calmed down enough to go to my room before someone from the conference saw me. Just about to walk into the elevator and there was his voice

screaming my name to answer, it was Larry run-

ning into the hotel lobby.

Chapter Seven

Thoughts raced through my mind so quickly now that I heard Larry's voice. My first thought was to get on the elevator and don't look back, and I did just that. With no hesitation, I leaped onto the elevator quickly so I wouldn't have to face Larry. Connor looked at me with confusion. "Kendall are you okay? Do you know that guy?" He asked with concern.

"Yes, please closed the door before he comes, I'll explain it later." I suddenly started feeling a sharp pain piercing through my body. Connor placed his hands on my shoulder. Just before the door closed, Larry pressed his hand against the door trying to stop it from closing. He continued to yell my name as the elevator door closed.

After we made it to my floor, we got off and Connor quickly stopped me. "Kendall will you tell me what's going on? Are you in danger?" He said looking at me in concern.

I sighed heavily and explained to him what was going on.

"Okay, so you're telling me your husband had his doctor friend steal your eggs doing the process you were using to was try to produce a child and use it on a surrogate which was his mistress? Now he wants you to take care of your daughter that he kept from you for three years because he's supposedly dying right?" He said, staring at me quizzically.

"Yes, and I don't think I can handle this pain. At this point I just want him to die and get out of my life. I don't want to hate him, but the things he is doing to me are so evil I can't stand to be in same room with him," I told him as I inserted my room key in the door.

"Look Kendall you're going to get through this. I will be right by your side and helping you in the best way I can. No strings attached." He said as he was trying to comfort me.

"Thank you," I replied to him. Within an hour he left after he had seen that I was fine, and Larry wasn't coming to the room. Suddenly my phone started ringing beside me. Without even looking at who was calling, I answered it.

"Hello,"

"Why are you still running, I'm trying to get this matter settled," I heard Larry say on the other end of the phone.

"Are you seriously asking me this question?" I said.

"Look, Kendall it wasn't planned like this," he said with compassion in his voice.

"Larry, take your money, all your assets, I don't want nothing but my child, and you will be hearing from my lawyer." I said, then hung up the phone. My inner self screamed, God has your back, you're not alone. I looked at myself in the mirror on the wall in the room and said: "Do not let my heart be drawn to what is evil so that I take part in wicked deeds along with those who are evildoers."

<><><><>

Then, I went and sat on the bed, trying to collect all my thoughts. My head was throbbing thinking of how unfathomable it was the way my life had changed from being a mother of one child to becoming a mother of two girls with a path of courts, laws and battles filled with misery to come.

The pain seemed never ending with Larry, and I didn't know if we would ever be able to mend what he has broken because this has become too deep. As I coasted over to look out the window to view the beauty of the city, I could only think of the little girl and the drastic changes on how my life going to be from here. Groaning, then shook my head realizing that this is all in God's plan and remembering that this is His WILL, His WAY, and my FAITH.

Suddenly my phone rang, bringing me out of my deep thoughts. I briefly glanced over at the name on the screen and it was Carol calling me. I reached over and grabbed the phone and answered it.

"Hello Ken, this is Carol." Listening to her voice, it sounded like she was crying.

"Are you alright? Do you need anything?" I asked Carol.

"I need to leave here. It's too much, Ken."

"Leave where?" I asked, wanting to be clear and certain of what was going on.

"This house, this marriage thing is not working for me. Scott and I can't get along."

Immediately I began to try to calm Carol down. She told me that it was time for her and Scott to move on, and that the only way for her to forget him she had to sleep with Charles Dennis, Scott's friend from high school.

As I talked things over with Carol, I convinced her to confess to Scott and make things right between them, because life is too short and he's a good man. Then finally we ended the phone call and I took a hot shower to relax the

rest of the night.

Chapter Eight

It was dark, and the smell of gasoline was rising in my nostrils. I opened my eyes and I was in this big old house, tied up to a chair. Searching around to see how I got tied up, all I could hear was the echo from my voice screaming for help. Suddenly, a light came on and Isabella walked out of a small room wearing all black and gloves. She walked toward me and laughed, mocking me. I glanced over at Isabella, asking her what she was doing, but she turned her back to me and walked over to flip on the lights. When the light was on, Larry was tied up in a chair. Every bone in my body was burning with fire with anger. I looked over at Larry and he looked at me with this vulnerable look, pleading for help. He immediately started yelling at Isabella, begging her to let me go. Isabella started yelling back at him and the argument began back and forth. Then Isabella pulled out a gun from the back of her jeans and shot Larry with no hesitation in the chest. Fear enveloped me as I saw Larry's body fall backward to the floor. I glanced at Isabella and she ran over and slapped me right in the head with the tip of the gun. I could see death right before my eyes.

"You ruin everything for me. We were supposed to get married, but Larry just couldn't let you go. Now death will do you part." She replied as she began pacing back and forth.

"You're going to pay for the pain your husband caused me, I hate you!"

I screamed to try to stop her and all I saw was a bright light and the gun staring two inches from my head. Isabella squeezed the trigger and I screamed. I leaped out of that terrible dream and ran to the bathroom continuing to splash water on my face. As I looked in the mirror, I could still see the fear of how real that dream seemed. Flashing back on the dream again, I was shaken out of my thoughts when the ring tone of my phone sounded. I walked into the room and got the phone. I picked it up and looked to see who was calling--Scott. I answered it.

"Kendall, please talk to Carol. She's around here sleeping with Branford in my house. I'm done with this selfish, undeniably ruthless friend."

"Okay, Scott calm down and let me speak to Carol, "I said as I searched for my belongings to get dressed for the conference.

Carol got on the phone yelling and arguing with Scott. It was the longest twenty minutes I had ever talked to someone on relationships. Then I began to remind them that relationships can't work without communicating.

Finally, I ended the call and finished getting dressed to head to the conference. Thinking back on what a crazy morning I've had so far, I knew that it was all distraction to kill my spirit. So, I said a silent prayer and then entered the elevator. When I got onto the elevator, there was a woman and her daughter in it as well. The little girl was so pretty and then I spoke to them. I began to miss my baby girl even more. The elevator stopped and we exited off it; they began to follow me toward the conference.

"You going to the conference here too?" The lady asked me."Yes, I am, looks like we have something in common." I said.

"Yes, the speaker is dynamic, and she's been through a lot, I've been to every one of her conferences." She said as she chuckled.

"Yes, I know her personally."

"Really? That is great,"

"Well let me introduce myself. I'm Ms. Alexandra." I said as I flash a smile to the woman. She hugged me and began telling me how she had been wanting to meet in person. I entered the conference and spoke to hundreds of women. The spirit of unity was in the atmosphere.

<><><><><><>

After it was over, I saw him staring at me the whole time. He walked over to me gazing into my eyes.

"Hello superstar, can I borrow you as a date tonight?" He asked with a huge smile. I looked over and gave him a smile.

"Are you going to return this borrowed superstar?"

"It all depends if she's amazing or not, and if she is just as I imagine and have seen so far. It's going to be really hard to return her."

"Okay, I'll think she might just take the risk." I replied.

He chuckles. "But I have the feeling she might just need a night out more than me."

He grabbed one of my hands and kissed it on the top.

"Well I'll see you at 8am."

I could feel the heat from his body when he kissed my hand. With his soft lips touching my hands, the smell of his polo black cologne scent and the feel of his breath on my skin had me shivering on the inside from the heat rising and running all the way down my inner body core. Trying to swallow hard and ignore this amazing feeling, I just moved away to ensure that I'll be ready. I started walking toward the elevator to go back to my room and Larry came out of nowhere.

"You've been here three days and already going on dates with strangers?" Larry said with his eyes narrowed, staring at me.

"Stay away from me, what I choose to do is my business."

He glared back at me, "Excuse me?"

Feeling the sense of a big disagreement and argument coming, I quickly leaped onto the elevator before someone from the conference saw us.

"You can't tell me who I can and can't talk to or go on a casual dinner with." I turned to leave the elevator, but Larry grabbed my arm and swung me toward him.

"You belong to me, besides that guy is not right for you. I can sense it."

"Let me be the judge of it. One thing for sure I know he's not like you so that is a great advantage. Now get your filthy hands-off me." I said angrily as I snapped away from him.

Larry punched his fist against the wall of the elevator. The fact that I didn't fear him anymore was driving him crazy.

"Kendall, I just want to settle everything and talk to you. Please get past the bitter attitude."

Looking up at him in defiance, "I'll talk to you when I have the time, now good-bye Larry,"

I said and then open the elevator door to walk to my room. Putting his hand on the door he just stared at me. "It's important."

"You don't believe in important, I was never important to you."

"Gosh! For heaven's sake Kendall, are you going to ever forgive me?"

"I have, you just keep flaring it up."

"Darn it, Kendall do you know how crazy I am about you?"

Trying to ignore what he was talking about, Larry grabbed my arms, pressing tight to draw me closer to him.

"Yes, so crazy you couldn't be faithful through our marriage and jumped in the bed with another woman and got her pregnant."

Seeing his eyes watering up he wrapped his arms around me, and his lips came forcing down on mine. Crushing my lips, he ravished my mouth as he pushed my body into his. For a quick moment I felt swept away by the heat of the moment. But then reality kicked in and I shoved him away.

Chapter Nine

I took a restless nap, thinking about the audacity of Larry's actions with that kiss. Confused by what he was thinking, I was distracted by the alarm clock I set before my nap to alert me to get ready before Connor arrived. It was now seven p.m., so I quickly got dressed.

I knew I was overwhelmed and cautious when it became to my relationships. After a failed marriage, and the relationship with Scott producing a child in the midst, the odds felt decidedly against me. That fear of love had overpowered me. I'd learned that in relationships it's necessary to use all five senses--the way they touch, smell, taste, look and feel. Each encounter with people in your life is a lesson, blessing or lifetime.

So, meeting Connor the way I did seemed very real to me. He was the type of guy a woman dreamed and prayed daily about but getting to know him better would determine if he was really worth it.

Nerves fluttered in my belly. It had been two years since I'd been in the dating scene, but I believed this was my season to find love. Still, knowing how thin the line between love and fear could have caused me to question if it was real or not.

As I got dressed, sliding on a beige dress and red pumps, then curling my hair, I was finally satisfied with my look. I just hoped Connor would agree. Waiting for him to arrive, I called my baby girl to see how she was doing. We talked for a while and she danced, sung, and read to me the whole time. Every moment with her was truly such an enjoyment. A knock sounded at the door and I finished up the call with her and hung up. With no hesitation I assumed it was Connor and opened the door. On the other side was an unfamiliar guy holding a bundle of roses in his hands.

"Ms. Alexandra?" He asked as he reached to hand me the roses.

"Yes, it is," I responded, looking confused.

"These are delivered by a very special guy to a very special woman."

"Well thank you, may I ask who?" I asked, but before I could get my words out, all of a sudden Connor come from around the corner with three other guys following him with instruments. He began singing the very own Kem song entitled 'It's You'.

I was shocked but filled with joy knowing this was one moment I'd never forget. Once he had finished singing, Connor stood in front of me with a breath that gasped from his lips looking at me in the way I took his breath away. All we both could do was just stand there staring.

"Wow Kendall, you look very beautiful." He finally said to me.

I blushed as I saw the way he looked at me. Connor lightly kissed me on the cheek.

<><><><><><>

"You look absolutely lovely." He grabbed my hand.

"Cheer up; it's okay for someone to be your mirror to remind you how amazing you can be."

"You shouldn't have, this is just beautiful." I stated, gazing in his eyes. I wanted to kiss him so badly, but I refuse to let my desire overpower me this time.

"Well this is just the beginning, now let's go."

"Okay, this is amazing, you're amazing Mr. Collins."

"You're not bad yourself, Ms. Alexandra"

He then kissed my hand and we exited my room and headed toward the elevator to get to the hotel lobby. As we entered the lobby area there was a gleaming white limo and a driver waiting beside the door. Immediately, we climbed in and closed the door. It was amazing, not knowing what else to expect from him.

"Please, Connor, you don't have to be prince charming. This is wonderful, you don't have to try so hard. I've been in relationships with the richest and expensive things doesn't impressed me. I just want you to be yourself and not go over and beyond for me."

Connor looked over at me with sincere seriousness covering his expressing. He chuckled.

"Oh, it's so sweet for you to think this was just for you, but the Director of The Reginald WMC Conference made arrangements for me. So, I decided to just let you ride with me." He said with a grin on his face, and then he burst out with this laugh. I looked at him feeling embarrassed at the moment and shook my head.

"Seriously."

"Yes seriously. No, I'm just kidding Ms. Kendall. I am not trying hard because this is in my nature for me to treat a woman with royalty. My grandmother once told me, you have one opportunity to show a woman your heart, so make the best of it. I might not ever be able to show you an another night like this, taking you to luxury restaurants and treating you as the queen you are, but I will make sure that you will never forget this moment and with that I will love the hell out of you until I am able to repeat it over and over again. You, and every woman, are priceless, so I don't want the discount. I want to pay full price even if I have to work the rest of my life to earn you. I don't have all the money in the world, but I have something that money can't buy and that's love I can offer you." He finished, staring in my eyes. This man was just too polite. Connor shifted backed against the seat in the car so he can stare at me directly.

"There is a feeling I have for you that is so strong, I can't place an exact name on it, but you make me want to just make you smile every day. I don't know what all you been through in your life, but there is never a moment I want to see you cry and if you do, I want to be the one to wipe your tears from your face."

Looking at him even more in shock, I just couldn't believe a man like Connor felt that way about me.

"You really feel that way?" I asked him, staring with wonder.

"Yes, because I like the fact that I am feeling this way and even more grateful that it's you that makes me feel like this. Because to me, from your head to your toes, you're perfect just for me. Ms. Kendall you make me want to do everything the right way."I stared at him and suddenly, my lips began pressing against his and we slowly start kissing."You really are amazing."

"Nah! I'm alright," Connor said, closing the space between us and he kissed me back. Once we pulled back from one another, there was a

gleaming smile on both of our faces.

Chapter Ten

After riding around New York viewing the skylines, Times Square, parks and other attractions, we finally made it to the restaurant. As we walked in the building, their were people greeting us all the way until we sat down. This was by far the best fine dining restaurant I'd ever been to and Larry had taken me to some nice elegant ones that millionaires visit, but they weren't anywhere near as good as this one. I began to think that moments are not measured by the amount of dollars that were spent, but by the energy you share at the moment. This restaurant had a waiting area, which was amazing. It had a lover's lounge where music was playing softly; a server was circulating with strawberries and wine. Artists painted photos while waiters tossing hearts to each other, then they would give the hearts to the couples. Inside the hearts they had love quotes catering to couples and once they received the heart, they had to be creative with the quote. I witnessed one man singing a quote to his date, and then another couple was dancing to a quote. This moment was just amazing, unforgettable, and it was well needed for me. Finally, we were seated and began to order our dinner. While eating, Connor and I began to get to know one another more. I learned that he had a son that was nine years old, living with his mother in Mobile Alabama. He'd been in one marriage that was chaotic to him. His Ex was a heavy gambler, and their marriage was ruin after he finished med-school and became a gastroen- terologist she gambled away their savings. He was raised by his grandmother and grandfa- ther after his mother was murdered by his fa- ther, due to domestic violence. They're God- fearing Christians who lived about five blocks from him in Florida.

Listening to Connor, I really realized that he is not a bad guy at all. He'd been through a lot, just like me and God is his backbone to his trial and triumph. We laughed, joked around and ate. After two hours spent endlessly talking, we finally left the restaurant. Suddenly my phone started ringing. I grabbed it to see who it was and, of course, it was Larry calling. Quickly I just threw it back in my purse; I wasn't going to let Larry ruin my night with his nonsense. We walked outside and there was a karaoke bar across the street from the restaurant. Connor looked at me with sparks in his eyes.

"Let's do it." He prompted, pointing toward the bar. "Let's go to the karaoke bar, it wouldn't be a fun night without ending it with a little wild fun."

"No, I can't, I am not a singer and no way I'm going to make a fool of myself."

He slipped his hands into mind, beginning to drag me toward the bar. "No one knows you here and I'll do all the work, let go." He said as he squeezed my hands a little. I submitted to his request and then we walked over to the bar.

We entered the bar; it was big and tall with a unique Southern style to it. Connor loved the interior of the bar while we surveyed around the space. Flashing lights came on the center stage and the host came out calling for the next round of participants to sing. Immediately, Connor raised his hand up and notified them that he was ready to try.

The host signaled for him to come and everyone began staring at the both of us. I found a seat to watch everyone. Some were laughing, some talking, some just enjoying the moment, which made me feel a little more comfortable. I felt like

I'd stepped into another world, but it was a good one. The kind that felt like you were living. Sometimes we can get so caught up in this Christian life we forget to just live. We will find ourselves not enjoying moments and forget that God would want us to live an abundant life which means create memorable moments, have fun, enjoy what he created, but still honor the creator. Connor walked up on the stage and grabbed the microphone; before I could get good and seated, he called for me to come up. I looked at him and whispered across the room telling him "NO!"

He kept insisting, however, that I come up there with him. Finally, I complied, and walked up there in a nervous wreck.

"Wow." I said as I looked at him.

"Yes wow, I wasn't going to leave you out of this fun." He replied with a soft smile.

"I can't say I did not see this coming." I smiled back and then the music started playing. The song came across the screen and it was (Marvin Gaye & Tammie Terrell, "Ain't No Mountain High Enough") which I was satisfied because that was one of the greatest hits that I loved. By eleven thirty, I was getting tired and we finally climbed inside the limo and headed to back to the hotel. We arrived at the hotel and climbed out the limo. Connor started to walk me to my room.

"Thank you for tonight, it was amazing, and I really had fun." I whispered to him.

"I'm glad you had fun, you deserve the best." Connor said as he leaned up against me. He started running his hands through my hair softly then wrapped then around my neck.

"Will I see you again?"

"Yes, of course, I will see you again." The feeling of fear came across me, wondering if this will be the ending to my mini fairy-tale.

Connor kissed me on the forehead and walked away, wishing me a good night sleep over his shoulder as he did. I then inserted my room key inside the door and entered it. Lord behold Connor kissed me on the forehead and walked away, wishing me a good night sleep over his shoulder as he did. I then inserted my room key inside the door and entered it. Lord behold Larry was sitting on the sofa while the little girl was lying across the bed.

Chapter Eleven

"**H**eaven's SAKE! Larry what in living JESUS is going on?" I yelled with anger. Larry jolted up from the sofa, rushing to put his hands over my mouth.

"Kendall please, calm down! I need you to keep her for the night." He said in a soft voice.

"Why? No Larry I will not. How did you get inside my room?"

"That's not the main reason Kendall. I just told the front desk you're my wife and I lost my key."

"This is ridiculous, how dare you think you can come in and out my life like you still own me? This is unfair, and especially unfair to this innocent child."

Larry looked at me with seriousness across his face. "Kendall, I understand you're angry with me, or even hate me, but this innocent child is our blood, your daughter. There is nothing I can do that will make you forgive me for keeping her away from you for three years, but she knows you more than you know yourself. She knows you as her mother, I always kept you close to us even though you were far away. I guess I can say God knows how to bring the truth to light especially for his own."

As he was speaking, I wanted to grab something heavy and just knock him unconscious, but reality kicked in my mind that what he was saying made sense. I can't blame the child for the evilness of her father and of course she is my daughter, though she was birthed by another woman.

"Yes, I guess two wrongs don't make a right. Can you please tell me why you did it? Larry why?" He sighed heavily and walked close toward me. I quickly warned him to back off and not to come any closer.

"Kendall, can we discuss this on a different occasion, because I have to get going. I am so sorry." He stated as he handed over the little girl's toys.

"No. I will not keep her until you tell me why." I returned firmly.

"Please, not now Ken?" Larry begged.

"If not now, then when? I can't keep her."

"You have to; I have no one else I trust. You are her mother, whether you want to admit it or not."

"Wow, after three years you expect me to be super mom and know everything about her. At least tell me her name." I said, feeling my body blazing up from the frustration and anger. It made me wonder all over again how I once was married to a selfish man like him.

"Her name is Kendra, Kendra Alexandra. Yes, like our other baby Ken." Immediately tears start flowing down my face and I slap him before I knew it. I couldn't believe what I was hearing. For him to name her after our other daughter that died seems to be so cruel to me. Not to say that it was his intention, but I know Larry was really hurt about the death of Ken, and that was the main reason that lead him back to drinking heavily. We both were so broken, but I would never in a lifetime name another child after her because, she still existed no matter what.

"Kendra like Ken, right? How could you Larry?" I asked him.

"Yes, but I am so sorry Kendall, Damn! I didn't deserve that slap. If I tell you why, will you keep her please?"

"I am waiting, explain."

"Well, I promise it wasn't supposed to play out like this. When we kept going back and forth to the doctor, I asked my buddy to steal your eggs. After the last visit and they stated that you weren't going to be able to carry a full pregnancy, I couldn't wait anymore. All my life I just wanted a real family with children, and you could not give that to me. So, I went to the doctor's office one day and checked to see what other option we could do, and Isabella was there. She was waiting on another couple to be their surrogate. We started talking and I told her our situation and she agreed to be our surrogate. The next day I just called up Dr. Oscar and explained to him what I wanted to do and how I wanted to surprise you on the whole plan. The day I was going to tell you I took Isabella to dinner, and one thing lead to another. I began to fall for her knowing she was carrying my baby now. I never loved her, I always loved you. It was all for you, and when our marriage became rocky, I ran to her, spent time with her. I became controlling against you because I didn't want you to find out the affair and leave me. When you saw us at the hospital, and I saw you with that guy, I knew it was over. So, I packed my bags and we moved to New York. I was going to tell you one day but didn't know when. Kendall, I love you so much and I never meant to hurt you."

"Wow, I just can't believe what I am hearing. You had some nerve Larry. That is illegal. How could you do that? I forgive you, but I hope you know that this doesn't make up for the fact of what you and Isabella have done. You can go now. I'll keep her, please just go."

Larry stared at me for a few minutes looking scared, knowing he messed up and consequences for his evil deeds would be coming soon.

"Thank you. She likes banana, and she's a very intelligent little girl. She loves to be independent." He rambled as he walked out the door.

"Yeah! I'm sure she is." I replied, a bit hollowly.

As he walked out the door, I followed him and was about to close it and he held it open. He began telling me he was coming back tomorrow to get her, and he had a scheduled outpatient surgery in the morning.

 I walked in the room and sat on the edge of the bed, glancing over at Kendra, looking at her up close the first time. She was the little girl in my dream on the plane. She had the prettiest long hair, French braided, bronze skin and the curliest eyelashes. She was a little angel. I knelt and kissed her on the cheek and then took off my shoes, took a warm shower, prayed and climbed in the bed beside her and I was soon sound asleep.

112

Chapter Twelve

I woke up from the bright light of the sun beaming through the curtains in my hotel room window. I yawned with slothfulness and turned over to see if Kendra was awake. I looked over and she wasn't there, causing me to immediately jump up with the urgency and fear of not knowing where she was. I ran toward the dining area of my suite and all the sudden she jumped out of the mirror closet.

"Peek a boo mommy!" She said with biggest smile on her face. I didn't know how to respond to her calling me mommy, as playful as joyful as she was.

"Peek a boo," I said back to her as I reached and grabbed her, tickling her on the sides.

"I missed you Mommy, Daddy said you were coming to get me when you done with work!" She said while hugging me tightly around my neck.

"I missed you too baby girl, we have so much to catch up on." I replied and then kissed her on the cheek. I asked if she was hungry and then ordered some room service for us. While waiting on them to arrive she started watching the cartoon network. I went back in the room to call Scott to speak with Destiny, but she was at the day-care. Scott and I began to chat about him and Carol agreeing to take counseling for their marriage, and he was explaining that his Aunt will be calling me more about the case. Suddenly a knock sounded at the door--the room services. I ended my phone call with Scott and Kendra, and we ate our breakfast. It was now Saturday and I'd planned to go back home Monday. I bathed her and put her on some clothes until Larry came by. Two hours had passed and Larry still hadn't texted or called to see how Kendra was doing or even tell me when he was coming to get her. So, I grabbed my phone and called Connor, asking if he could take us to the park so Kendra would have something to do. Of course, he was all for it, I hurried and got dressed so we can head to the hotel lobby to meet him. While waiting in the room, Kendra was coloring in her activity book, and then she began to tell me Isabella had been mean to her and that she was always arguing with her daddy. As she was telling me that, I started thinking on how I could speed the process of getting full custody of her, because that was the absolute last thing I wanted for an environment for my child. A sense of unease came in my spirit, knowing that she'd have to go back to that. She asked about Destiny and told me that her dad told her about her other sister. I had to listen clearly for everything she was saying, but she still was super smart and intelligent for her age. Very aware and alert, which amazed me about her. Thanking God in my spirit, trying to unravel everything on why now I find out about this wonderful, beautiful little angel. There was a knock at the door that drifted me away from my thoughts. I leaped to answer, and it was Connor.

I grabbed our items and Connor helped assist with Ken's things so we could head to the elevator.

Once I made it to the hotel lobby, Connor went to go grab the car as we patiently waited. My phone rang then, and I pulled it from my purse quickly. I answered the call from an unknown number. It was a woman on the other end of the phone, and as the words came out of her mouth my heart felt like it had dropped out of my chest.

Larry had been shot by his girlfriend, and she was saying he was in critical condition. The shooter was on the run, known to be his ex-fiancée.

"Lord have Mercy," I whispered.

Chapter Thirteen

My body had became so numb that my phone slipped out my hands and glided to the chair. I started praying to myself as my spirit became vulnerable to the actions on how Ken will respond. Connor came inside the hotel to tell us he had the car ready. I looked over at him and told him the situations, thinking he would be upset that I cancelled our outing because of my ex-husband. Connor was very supportive and understood everything well, though. We got into the car and headed to the hospital, my heart pumping while thoughts kept running through my head. How would things be for Ken if Larry didn't make it through this and how would I adjust my life to that? On our way traveling there, Connor kindly offered to watch Ken until I could check on Larry and his status. He reached over and gripped my hand tight. "It's going to be okay, God is in control," He said reassuringly.

After twenty minutes of driving, we finally arrived at the hospital. The last time I rushed to a hospital like this, I was with Scott coming to check on his mother, and that was the day everything in my life changed. Feeling a little deja vu, I wondered if this would signal another drastic change in my life.

We approached the floor where Larry was, and his Uncle Mason stood up to greet us.

"I am glad you made it Kendall, it looks bad." He said bluntly.

"How is he? And what happened?"

Mason sat back down as he took a sip of his coffee and breathed a heavy sigh.

"Isabella shot him three times in the back, after an argument for her to leave Larry's home."

"That's absurd, why would she do that?"

"Isabella is out of control and Larry just couldn't deal with it anymore."I couldn't believe what I was hearing; it was so shocking to me. I looked at Connor, hurt and angry at the situations. He called for Ken to go with him while I went to check on Larry. Then, I walked inside his hospital room to stand over him, helpless and still unconscious. Reaching over to grab his hand, I murmured a silent prayer before kissing him on the forehead and heading for the door.

Several minutes later he opened his eyes, struggling weakly to tell me he was sorry. He turned his head, glancing at me. "Take care of our baby."

"It's okay, I will. You just get better, I need you to get through this for Ken and me. That little girl out there needs her father." I replied, tears beginning to fall down my cheeks. A headache was pounding between my temples.

"Can I please see my baby?" Larry asked as he gasped for breath.

"Sure, I'll go get her."

I stepped outside the door and signaled for Connor to bring her to me. She ran over to me and I picked her up and walked inside the room.

"Daddy, you sick?" She asked him as she stood beside him holding his hand.

"Yes, Daddy real sick and it will be awhile before you see Daddy. You're going to be with Mommy for a while."

"Okay, I'm going to let my guardian angel protect you Daddy," Ken said, tears pooling in her pretty eyes. Larry couldn't stand to see her. He began to cry as well and start choking, grasping for breath.

I turned to walk out with Ken, but Larry grabbed my arm.

"Talk to Mason please,"

Looking confused and worried, I just nodded my head, assuring him I will talk to him. The nurse came rushing in to check on him and I quickly took Ken out the room.

"What's this about Larry wanting me to ask you something?" I asked Mason as I sat near him in the waiting room.

"Yes, he has the paperwork ready to sign over to you for all of his assets, but the paperwork will not be finalized until Monday."

"Mason my flight is meant to leave tomorrow, I don't think I'll be here."

"Oh, that's a shame. Larry went through a lot to get this transferred over to you and baby Ken."

Connor walked over toward us. "Kendall, if you need to stay longer, I am willing to drive you back or rearrange a flight for you."

"No, Connor you've done enough, and you don't have to stick around like this. What do you want from me?" I said, feeling over-whelmed about everything.

"I don't want anything but you. I am sticking around because this is what I want to do. Ken-dall, when people care about someone, that's what they do. They support them. You can try to run me off, but I am not going anywhere because I know you're the woman God made for me. So just quit brushing me off and accept my help."

"Okay, Kendall you better take advantage of this good man's offer." Uncle Mason told me firmly. Then, we all sat around waiting for Larry's nurses to let us know about him. Hours passed by and Ken was getting restless. Finally, the doctor came out to give us the news that Larry was in stable condition and that he will be here for a while.

"Kendall, you all can go ahead and get some rest, I will call if anything comes up." Mason stated as he strode toward me.

"Okay thanks, is it possible I can get the key to Larry's place to get some of Ken belongings?"

"Sure, perhaps it will be yours soon." Mason said as he reached in his pocket for the key. He handed me the key, and we headed out of the hospital.

Chapter Fourteen

Traveling twenty-five minutes out-side the city limit we arrive to Larry's mansion, and I suddenly begin to feel nervous. Visualizing the thoughts of how things went down and how familiar this house's design was to my previous, I didn't even notice that I had made it to the front door of the house. I pressed the doorbell just to see if anyone was there, but no one answered. So, I inserted the key, making my way inside, almost tripping over the shattered glass & clothing laying on the floor, items vandalized, and pictures broken, with empty wine bottles on the tables. Looking at everything, I could easily imagine the encounter Larry and Isabella had before the incident. Walking through the hallway and looking in every room trying to find Kendra stuff, I stopped to look in Larry room due to Kendra's stuff was all on the floor, so I assume her stuff was in his room. Making my way in the room the sight I found was one I wished I could have left unseen. Isabella was lying in the tub, dead. I could do nothing but scream. "God have mercy!" I screamed, then rushed out of the house to immediately call 911.

"She's dead, Isabella is dead in the tub!" I shouted to Connor. He jumped out of the car with urgency.

"Kendall! Kendall! Are you okay?" He asked, and then he grabbed me and held me close, understanding how horrific this situation is to me.

As much pain as she'd caused me, it still broke my heart to know that this woman just took her on own life. We waited until the police and ambulance arrive before I entered back into the mansion to get Kendra's belongings.

We spent twenty minutes being questioned by the police for their report, all the while Kendra was sleeping through the incident. At long last, we reached the hotel and I finally was able to get Kendra into bed. Connor stuck around after until I made all my phone calls.

As I walked to front area of my room, he was sound asleep on the sofa. He looked so amazing lying there, peaceful. Of course, I didn't want to wake him, so I covered him with a blanket and took a warm shower. I prayed for strength to make it through this severe test, thinking about how life isn't always sunshine and roses. Sometimes you just have to learn to smile through the pain.

Finally, I dozed off to sleep, hoping that I would have a better day tomorrow. I was awakened by my phone ringing, answering to find Uncle Mason notifying me that Larry was responding better to treatment and that he was looking for me.

Kendra was in the living room area watching TV. I surveyed around to see if Connor was in the other room, but he was nowhere to be found. Glancing over at the table beside the chair, there was a letter from Connor that read: "Good morning beautiful, I had to take off this morning for a meeting; I didn't want to wake you. But please give me call on my cell if you need me to make arrangements for you and baby girl.

Yours only, Connor"

 I felt sparks flaring up in my spirit as I read the letter. Just when I thought my life could get no better, God had a ram in the bush to brighten up my day. Even through my dark days I knew a man like Connor would make the light shine. Snatched out of my thoughts, Kendra walked over and sat on at lap.

"Mommy, will I see Daddy today?" I kissed her forehead and nodded.

"Yes, baby," I said softly, as I watched her continue to look at the cartoon channel.

I had now gotten used to occasional weird things happening in my life, but usually they were over quickly. This nightmare wouldn't go away. This has been the most dreadful seventy-two hours I've lived through.

Kendra and I slipped on some clothes for me to catch a cab downtown to the hospital to visit Larry. On our way out the hotel, of course by now the conference is over but word about Larry and what happen to Isabella had spread immediately. Wherever I went, people were pointing at me and murmured something about incident, because it was headline news due to Larry's status in the city. Finally, we made it to the hospital, and up to Larry's room.

"I've got paperwork to do," Mason said flatly. "Will you stick around for a while?"

"Sure, I can, but not too long. I have to get things prepared for travel."

"Okay great, I won't be long. You need to go talk to Larry. He's up." Mason said.

I nodded, assuring him I would do just that. Ken and I walked in the room and Larry had just finished eating his food, looking really weak in the face. For some reason I felt so vulnerable at that moment seeing him in that hospital bed, knowing that it could've been him dead instead of Isabella. Kendra ran over and gave Larry a big hug and kiss. He looked over at me and whispered that he was sorry. I immediately looked in his eyes and kissed him on the cheek. He looked at me skeptically, trying to understand if I was sincere or not.

"Please forgive me." He asked.

I lightly touched his shoulder, and he seemed to relax at the touch.

"It's alright. I am here Larry."

He grabbed hold of my hand and fell sound asleep. Kendra climbed in his bed and laid right beside him with her arms cuddled under him.

Chapter Fifteen

That was how I spent the rest of the day, patiently just waiting for Mason to come back. Sitting there, I searched though my purse to get my phone, but my hand came across the paper Larry had given me before all this happened. I sighed heavily and opened the paperwork, feeling hesitant to read it. I scanned the promissory notes, stating that Kendall Alexandra would have full authority over all property, and that half a million dollars would be put into my bank account.

I felt my heart racing.

"Oh, my lord, half million dollars?" Are you serious? Larry had to be crazy. Darn it! This can't be true. I felt hot, tears beginning to flow down my face that I couldn't hold back anymore. Drifting in a deep daze, I was interrupted by my phone's chirping text notification. It was Connor.

"Good morning love," he said.

"Good morning," I typed back immediately with a smiling face.

"I see you and baby girl made it out safe, you looked gorgeous this morning sound asleep." He stated, making me blush as I read the text.

"Connor, you're just amazing, thank you for everything."

"You're welcome. I will see you soon to discuss your traveling arrangements. Talk to you soon, beautiful."

I responded back with a simple "Okay."

Suddenly, Mason walked through the door and sat down to talk to me. We began to talk, and he covered the whole story behind everything. "Two weeks ago, Larry was diagnosed with cancer, and was told that he didn't have much time due to liver damage from his heavy drinking. His lawyer had advised him to do a quick claim deed to someone he trusted to continue his legacy and give them legal ownership of their property. Of course, Isabella was present when this was stated, and she assumed Larry would leave everything to her for Kendra. But when Larry found out you were in town, it was the great opportunity to make things right. He wanted to give you everything and announce your surprise daughter at the same time. Well, same week you arrived, Isabelle found the papers, trashed the house and got angry. She brought your daughter to the office and told Larry not to bring her near the house or him again or she will destroy them all. So, Larry thought the safest place for baby girl will be with her own mother, and that's when he brought her to your room."

"So that's why he came?" I asked.

"Yes, Isabella had threatened both of their lives."

"So, did he actually have surgery?"

"No, he didn't. He went to stay at the hotel and Isabella came there that next day and shot him."

I couldn't believe what I was hearing; thinking about how close that crazy manic had come to harming my daughter.

"So, I'm going to assume when she shot Larry, she thought he was dead, and that's why she committed suicide." I asked, curious.

"Yes, your guess is absolutely is right. She was young and her life was surrounding Larry and she gave a lot up for him, but her love she couldn't let go. But she has been getting therapy privately because Larry abused her mentally, physically and emotionally, which really doesn't justify her actions."

Mason and I talked for hours and then Larry woke, and I let him know that I was about to leave. It was a bittersweet love I had to show toward him because I love him as the father to my wonderful daughter I didn't know about, but nothing more. I grabbed Kendra and we headed out of the hospital to catch a cab back to the hotel. As we walked out, I saw Connor standing next to a car with his arms folded and a smile on his face.

"Good evening gorgeous, do you need a ride?" He said with an amazing smile. I looked at him and released a heavy sigh of relief that I didn't need to take a cab. If there is one thing that I love about him, it's that he is so wonderfully unpredictable. Every time I think he can't be more amazing he seems to amaze me more.

"Yes, we do sir," I said as I smiled at him. Kendra and I climbed inside the car and then Connor took us to grab something to eat.

I spent the rest of the day talking to lawyers and finalizing all of the paperwork so I can take my baby girl back home with me, Connor supporting me throughout.

Chapter Sixteen

It was one day away from me going back home and Larry was still in the hospital in critical condition. I was seriously contemplating taking up Connor on his offer of driving us back home. I made it to my room and kicked off my shoes, lying back, exhausted from the trials I have faced during my visit in New York City. A couple hours passed. Kendra was sound asleep, and I had talked to baby Destiny. I called for Connor to come down to my room so we can discuss what our arrangements would be. He arrived only twenty minutes later, and I opened the door. Without hesitation Connor grabbed hold of my neck, pulling my body close to his and began lavishing my lips as our mouths clashed.

My body burned and I wanted to pull back, but he kissed so well. Slowly, we made our way, pressing against the wall and then moving toward the couch. He grabbed hold of me so tight and pressed his chest against mine, the sensation growing quickly heated. I lightly pressed my hands on his chest which was so solid and tight. He continued to kiss the side of my neck, caressing my breasts, slowly sliding his fingers in between my inner thighs and stroking in and out of my vagina. The feeling was so amazing, it felt like deja vu. After caressing me softly, Connor picked me up and carried me to the bathroom. Upon entering the room, he sat me on top of the sink. Nerves came across my body knowing what about to happen. He stared me in my eyes and easily slid down my panties.

"Wait, we shouldn't do this, what if Ken wakes up?" I asked as I looked at him with sincerity.

"She won't, trust me," he smiled and immediately pressed his lips against my vagina. I tried to push him off, but he grabbed hold of my hand tightly with all his strength and continuing to lick me over and over again until I came.

"Are you okay?" He asked as he jolted up and kissed me on my neck.

I was in such a state of shock that all I could do is nod and continue to look at him.

He came over to help me off the counter and gave me a tight hug.

"You deserve that and more Kendall."

"Why?"

"Why not, I will fulfill all your needs spiritually, physically and emotionally. I can handle all of you if you will allow me."

"Wow! You are just amazing, but I don't think I am ready for commitment and a relationship right now." I said as I put on my panties.

"If not now, when? We met for a special reason and it is beautiful. I will never steer you wrong," He looked at me mysteriously while he reached over to turn on the bath water.

"Here, go ahead and clean up and then we will discuss our options." He said as he exited the room. My heart felt like it was on fire and I had no clue how to cool down. Then, I cleaned myself up and entered the living room area. He was sitting on the couch looking as handsome as ever.

We began to schedule things for the trip, and the conclusion was that we were going to leave in two days. We talked about his interests and spent a lot of time laughing at his jokes. I let out a breath of relief to know my trip was about to come to end and I could get back home. Connor had already made all of the arrangements, but he was just waiting on me to give the go ahead to proceed.

After a good hour and half, Connor left my room and gave me a long kiss goodbye.

I walked in the bedroom to check on Kendra, finding her sound asleep. I had never just stared at her so long. She looked like her father there, in a peaceful state. I bent over and lightly packed her on the forehead and lay down to sleep.

Chapter Seventeen

Two days passed, and it was time for us to start packing to get on the road. Larry was now out of ICU, awake and alert. We went by the hospital to let Kendra see her father, but I reached the 5th floor, I found crowds of reporters and police officials. Looking from a distance, I tried to move away from crowd and get to Larry's room. They started rushing toward me with haste.

"Ms. Alexandra how do you feel that your husband is under investigation for first degree murder of his alleged fiancée?" A news reporter asked, holding a recorder. Lights started flashing and I pushed through the crowd, ignoring what they were saying.

I saw Mason from a distance waving for me to come. I sped up, walking to him and we moved into Larry room.

"Kendall, it's a big mess, Larry is being charged with Isabella's murder. They're saying he hired someone to kill her and then turned himself in because he didn't pay him for the job." Mason was breathing hard, speaking with a sense of urgency. I was in shock to hear the news, but not surprised. That was what Larry did--he hired people to do the dirty work for him. Karma had arrived and she was making her presence known in Larry's life. No good ever came from bad intentions. So now he found himself caught up in several charges, not to mention the scandal move with stealing my embryo.

Larry was sitting up in bed, his eyes widening upon my arrival while Lil Kendra ran up to him and gave him a huge hug. He held her tightly, and tears started flowing down his eyes.

"I messed up, Kendall, I messed up" Larry said as he stared at me, teary eyed.

"What have you done, why?"

He looked over to Mason and asked him to take Kendra out so he could have a moment with me.

Mason picked Kendra up and they headed out the door, leaving Larry to look at me mysteriously.

"I am so sorry for everything I've done to you, I really am." He said, sniffling.

"It's okay, you're in a lot of disarray and chaos Larry."

"Please don't tell them about Kendra. Just go to the bank and empty out the account and take it. I will be gone for a while."

"How can I do that?" I sputtered.

"Your name is on the account, I made arrangements this morning." He responded quietly. "I'm friends with the manager at the bank."

"Hmm, friends like sleeping with her?"

"No, Kendall, it's not that, not everything I do has a hidden motive, you know."

"Sure, tell it to someone who doesn't know you."

"Please give me a break; do you not see my damn situation?"

"Yes, I do Karma is kicking your ass. Excuse my French, but we have nothing else to talk about."

I said bluntly as I walked toward the door to the leave the room.

"Really, you're still bitter as hell? You caused all this in my life. I gave you a life that you didn't even deserve. Why you just couldn't do like the other upper-class wives when they find dirt on their spouse? Deal with the shit and keep spending their money. All I wanted was for you to give me a child. You couldn't do that, so I had to steal one from you that cost me now."

As he was talking, I just wanted to strangle him to death. He was so vicious and a situation like this couldn't even stop his deceiving ways.

"How could you, Larry?" I snapped. "You deserve everything that's happened to you. One thing for sure, I am a firm believer that you will reap everything you sew, and you will look back and wonder why you gave me all your property and asset when you're lying in a jail cell. And when you do, remember I serve a God who will make my enemy my footstool. You are like a piece of furniture, you will live the rest of your life a supporting me elevating my steps to success. So farewell, Mr. Alexandra."

I walked out the door and it felt so good to know that everything I prayed for is coming to pass. God is our refuge and strength and if we let him fight our battles he will show up and show out. Going out the door, I grabbed Kendra to head out the hospital. Connor was waiting on us, so I quickly explained to him what was said and what Larry had done. On our way to the bank, I talked with Scott, letting him know when we will arrive and to inform Destiny that her sister coming home to her. After twenty minutes transferring all of

Larry's assets, we gathered all our items and got on the road, traveling back home.

Chapter Eighteen

It had been one month since I returned home. The road trip with Connor and baby Kendra was unforgettable. We laughed, we stopped at beaches, we enjoyed every moment. It took us a day and half to make it back on the Gulf coast. Upon our arrival, Scott had a surprise welcome party for Kendra. Connor and I were officially dating, and deeply in love. That trip to New York was a life changing event for me. With the power over Larry's assets I opened trusts and college funds for the kids, and a Center for young adults. Life was looking so great for me. One the day of my grand opening, Connor proposed to me in front of the media and hundreds of people. It was such an amazing day.

Kendra and Destiny are now the best of friends. A couple months have passed, and now I am full time working my business with Connor right by my side every step of the way. We've been in and out of courts with Larry, now that he's out of hospital and trying to reclaim all his assets. With his power and wealth, his family still bailing him out of trouble, but he is now under investigation for the case against me.

Finally, after six full months of custody battles and trying to prove my case against Larry, the judge was able to declare him guilty. At that moment it was bittersweet to see the father of my child go to prison, but I learned a long time ago that if you live by the sword, you'll die by the sword. Of course, he tried everything he could to destroy me before his final sentences.

A year passed and it's April 3rd—Connor's and I wedding day. I was inside my penthouse, while Kendra and Destiny were getting dressed up by Carol.

It was at that time that my wedding planner asked me to get ready to come out. As I walked out to the aisles of this amazing walkway, beautiful flowers were everywhere, draping of angels, pillows filled with blossom roses. I felt like I was walking through heaven's door. Crowds of families and friends filled the seats and there he was standing in all white. Connor looked like a handsome angelic human being. He was so fine it hurt my eyes to look at him. Well, maybe not, but it was literally the best moment ever.

Tears continue to flow down my face, unstoppable because for the man of my dreams, both of my babies here with me, and for me to stand here with my health and strength I owe God all the glory.

I got to the alter and we exchanged vows. Then, what a celebration it was.

As we celebrated at the reception, entertaining all of our guests, I went to my guest room to get out of my clothing. I pulled my clothing off and when I turned around to fix my hair the reflection in my mirror was one, I certainly was not prepared for, or rather who. It was cold-blooded, crazy Isabella, holding a gun pointed right at me.

"I am going to get back to get what belongs to me." She said.

Author

Erica T Capri

Erica T Capri is the author behind A Thin Line Trilogy Series. She is a stylist, film producer, entrepreneur, and playwright. Her work as playwright has become popular over the years with her production performing at Colleges and theatre stages. She's the rock star mother of two young children and COO of Gemlight Publishing LLC. Erica wrote over twenty pieces in the combination of stage plays, screenplays, children fiction, and novels. She has no plans to stop writing and hard at work on her book and film releases.

Follow the Author:

Facebook: Author Erica T Capri

Linkedin: Erica T Sherrill

Email: ericasherrill77@gmail.com

Interested in joining our Gemlight Publishing
family? Visit our website for more details!

Follow Us on Social Media ;
Facebook,Instagram,LinkedIn,& Twitter

www.gemlightpublishing.com

Gemlight Publishing LLC Company
Attn: Erica T Sherrill /COO
gemlightpublishingllc@gmail.com
49 Hardy Court, Suite 385
Gulfport, MS 39507
833-436-5483 /Cell

To Purchase more books visit:;
www.gemlightpublishing.com

Upcoming Title;

"Prayers for the Prey(Women's Em-
powerment)

"Today Is The Day !"(Children's Fiction)

"How to Invest To Be Bless"(Self-help)